The
Big Custard
Disaster

'The Big Custard Disaster'
An original concept by Heather Pindar
© Heather Pindar

Illustrated by Darshika Varma

Published by MAVERICK ARTS PUBLISHING LTD

Studio 11, City Business Centre, 6 Brighton Road,

Horsham, West Sussex, RH13 5BB

© Maverick Arts Publishing Limited February 2021

+44 (0)1403 256941

A CIP catalogue record for this book is available at the British Library.

ISBN 978-1-84886-771-0

Maverick
publishing

www.maverickbooks.co.uk

White

This book is rated as: White Band (Guided Reading)

The
Big Custard
Disaster

By Heather Pindar

Illustrated by Darshika Varma

Chapter 1
- Monday -

The lunch hall at Hilldip Primary School is one of the quietest in the whole country.

Usually, the children and teachers love chatting and being noisy whenever they can.

But at lunchtime they only want to eat, because they love Mrs Higgins's food more than anything.

So when their head teacher, Mrs Standforth, wanted everyone to listen, she only had to tap her glass gently with a spoon. She didn't try to stop the children and teachers from eating of course. She talked over the sound of the hundreds of small chomping and slurping noises in the hall.

"I have something very serious to say. Our wonderful cook, Mrs Higgins, has to go away for a few days. She will be back on Friday afternoon. So that means our lunches on Tuesday, Wednesday, Thursday and Friday will not be cooked by Mrs Higgins."

Everyone stared.

"Yes, yes, I know this is upsetting news. We will all just have to be brave and help each other through this." Everyone nodded sadly and tried to look brave. "We have a cover cook coming to make the lunches. His name is Mr Chump."

At that moment, Mrs Higgins stomped across the hall and stood next to Mrs Standforth.

She folded her arms. She looked around at the teachers and children without smiling. She spoke slowly and clearly. "If anyone, **anyone**, makes a mess of my kitchen, I'll quit. If even one spoon is out of place when I get back, I'll walk out, and I'll never cook another lunch for Hilldip School."

The chomping and slurping noises stopped. The children gasped. The teachers looked at each other and slowly shook their heads.

Chapter 2
- Tuesday -

The cover cook, Mr Chump, missed his bus and arrived late on his first morning.

He soon cheered up when he walked into the kitchen. Everything sparkled and gleamed. Every pan, spoon and bowl stood neatly in its place.

"Perfect!" said Mr Chump to himself. "I can try out all sorts of meals in this kitchen."

For Mr Chump, cooking didn't just mean making meals. It meant... **ADVENTURE**.

Mr Chump didn't make ordinary meals. That would be too boring. No, Mr Chump liked to experiment. He liked to make meals that no one had ever made before.

Mr Chump looked in all the cupboards. Then he set to work.

Chapter 3
- Wednesday -

The lunch hall was filled with a damp and sour smell. The children in the lunch queue wrinkled their noses.

"It smells even worse than yesterday," said Jim quietly.

"And looks worse too," whispered his twin sister, Layla. "I thought the cabbage and orange pizza yesterday was the worst thing I'd ever eaten in my life. That cabbage smelt like

Dad's socks. But this! Beetroot and spaghetti burgers... yuck!"

"They're kind of soggy and crunchy and hot and cold all at the same time," agreed Jim. "But don't worry, it's **mushroom sponge** for pudding."

"Ha ha, very funny," said Layla. "But at least we can cover it in custard. That should hide the taste of those slimy mushrooms."

"Oh, there's no custard," said their teacher, Mr Verne, who was sitting opposite them. "I asked Mr Chump. He said he doesn't believe in it. He says custard is boring. And he forgot to order it."

"Right! Enough is enough!" said Jim, leaping to his feet. "I'm going to see Mr Chump about this right now!"

Layla watched Jim stomping down the steps to the kitchen. She could hear lots of people muttering and grumbling around her. She couldn't hear any chomping or slurping noises at all.

After lunch, Jim came back to class with a big smile on his face. "It's chaos in the kitchen. Mr Chump let me sort out the food orders. I've been on the computer and ordered custard - and a few other things."

Chapter 4
- Thursday -

It was late afternoon when they heard the rumbling outside. Mr Verne was talking about the South Pole and tried to ignore it. But when the shouting started, everyone rushed to the windows.

Two big tanker lorries had stopped at the top of the slope that led down to the kitchen. A short, stocky driver was yelling angrily at a tall skinny driver. Mr Verne and the children leaned forward to hear better.

"I've been bringing Hilldip their custard for nearly twenty years! They can't have ordered your custard: it's rubbish!" shouted the stocky driver.

"Well they did order my custard," shouted the skinny driver. "Maybe they decided your custard is rubbish."

CUSTARD
2GO.COM

The stocky driver's face went purple. "Alright then. Let's give them all of your custard. They can find out how rubbish it is for themselves." He stamped around to the side of the skinny man's custard lorry. He heaved on a big tap. With a loud slapping and gurgling noise, a stream of custard slid down the slope towards the kitchen door.

CUSTARD 2GO.COM

The skinny driver's face went purple too. He stamped around to the side of the stocky man's custard lorry. He heaved on the big tap. With a loud slapping and gurgling noise, another stream of custard slid down the slope towards the kitchen door.

"I do hope that custard doesn't make a mess of Mrs Higgins's kitchen," said Mr. Verne. "I wonder who ordered so much."

Everyone turned slowly and looked at Jim.

Chapter 5
- Friday -

The mess was still there the next morning! An emergency assembly was held at 10 o'clock.

"Jim is very sorry about ordering far too much custard," she said. "He is also sorry that the kitchen is ankle-deep in custard. Every drop must be cleaned up. It's only 4 hours before Mrs Higgins returns at 2 o'clock. We all know what will happen if we fail. I don't even want to think about life without Mrs Higgins's lunches." Everyone in the hall nodded.

"Our caretaker, Mr Tong, says we must not tip custard down the drains. It blocks them. Lunch will be custard. No, Mehmet, you can't have chips with it. Mr Chump said he doesn't believe in custard. He's gone home early."

"Chump's got the hump!" giggled Layla.

"Shh, Layla!" said Mrs Standforth. "Class 5 are scooping custard into bowls for lunch. But that won't use up all the custard. Layla and Jim are making a 'Trifle Tower' for Mrs Higgins. Please help carry the leftover mushroom sponge cake and as much custard as you can to the lunch hall. Take a bucket from Mr Tong. Everyone else... grab a pencil case, any pot or bag and...

...**HIDE THE CUSTARD!** I don't care where. Just hide it."

The whole school set to work. At lunch everyone ate at least two big bowls of custard. Jonathan Bagley ate five bowls, but he had to lie down in the library afterwards.

Little pots and bags of custard went into cupboards, desks, the bike sheds and the boot of Mr Verne's car.

The Trifle Tower was a bit wonky but almost as tall as Layla.

Mr Tong swept the last dollops of custard into his toolbox. Jim mopped the kitchen floor.

At two minutes to two, Mrs Standforth spotted Mrs Higgins parking her car.

Everyone was already waiting nervously in the hall. "Good afternoon, Mrs Higgins," they chanted as she walked in.

"What's this?" she said straight away, looking at the Trifle Tower.

"We made it for you!" said Layla.

"Hmm," said Mrs Higgins. "I hope it hasn't made a mess of my kitchen." She stomped off down to the kitchen. No one spoke. After what seemed a very long time, they heard Mrs Higgins stomping back up the steps.

"Is everything as it should be in your kitchen?" asked Mrs Standforth nervously.

"No," said Mrs Higgins. "Someone has ordered 44 tins of sprouts."

Everyone turned slowly and looked at Jim.

"They looked like mushy peas in the picture!" said Jim.

"So, Mrs Higgins," said Mrs Standforth quickly, "even though the kitchen isn't totally perfect..." She glared at Jim. "Do you think you might possibly, please, **please** stay?"

Everyone held their breath. Mrs Higgins looked up at the ceiling. She put her hands on her hips. "Oh, alright then," she said. "I'll stay."

Everybody in the room jumped up. They cheered, they stamped, they grinned and high-fived each other.

"Alright," said Mrs Higgins when the hall was quiet again. "Now I suppose I'd better taste this big trifle."

Layla silently handed Mrs Higgins a spoon. Mrs Higgins dug out a small lump of Trifle Tower. She smelled it. She tasted it. She wrinkled her nose.

The tower moved very slightly. The top started to slide. In a moment, it had toppled over. It covered Layla, Jim and Mrs Standforth in mushroom sponge and custard.

Mrs Higgins stared at the mess. She began to shake. Mrs Higgins was shaking with laughter. For a moment, the teachers and children stared in amazement. No one had ever heard Mrs Higgins laugh. Then they all began to laugh too.

That afternoon, the lunch hall at Hilldip School was one of the noisiest in the whole country.

The End

Book Bands for Guided Reading

The Institute of Education book banding system is a scale of colours that reflects the various levels of reading difficulty. The bands are assigned by taking into account the content, the language style, the layout and phonics. Word, phrase and sentence level work is also taken into consideration.

Maverick Early Readers are a bright, attractive range of books covering the pink to white bands. All of these books have been book banded for guided reading to the industry standard and edited by a leading educational consultant.

Pink
Red
Yellow
Blue
Green
Orange
Turquoise
Purple
Gold
White

To view the whole Maverick Readers scheme, visit our website at www.maverickearlyreaders.com

Or scan the QR code above to view our scheme instantly!